A WINTER'S NAP

by **Winston White**

illustrated by **Ellen Sloan Childers**

Barksbee
BOOKS

SILVER BURDETT & GINN

SILVER BURDETT & GINN

Simon & Schuster A Paramount Communications Company

BARKSBEE BOOKS and Colophon are trademarks of
Silver, Burdett & Ginn Inc.

Text © 1992 Silver, Burdett & Ginn Inc.
Art © 1992 Ellen Sloan Childers.

ISBN 0-663-54560-9

Developed by Cebulash Associates

2 3 4 5 6 7 8 9 10 WP 95 94 93 92

It was October. The days were growing shorter and colder. Winter was on its way.

Groundhog got his blanket, his pillow, and his alarm clock. He was just about to burrow deep into his den when Fox came by.

"There's some good fishing down at the old millpond," said Fox.

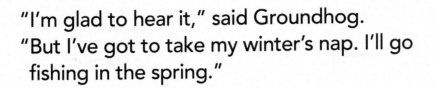

"I'm glad to hear it," said Groundhog.
"But I've got to take my winter's nap. I'll go
fishing in the spring."

"Sweet dreams," said Fox and off he went
to the millpond.

Groundhog was about to burrow deep into his den when Raccoon came by.

"There are some tasty berries in the woods by the creek," said Raccoon.

"I'm glad to hear it," said Groundhog.
"But I've got to take my winter's nap. I'll eat
  berries in the spring."

"Sweet dreams," said Raccoon and off he went
  to the woods.

Groundhog was about to burrow deep into his den
when Otter came by.

"There is some fine diving at the lake," said Otter.

"I'm glad to hear it," said Groundhog.
"But I've got to take my winter's nap. I'll go
 diving in the spring."

"Sweet dreams," said Otter and off he went
 to the lake.

Groundhog was about to burrow deep into his den. But he had been interrupted so many times and he was so tired that he fell asleep right then and there on the floor.

He forgot his blanket.
He forgot his pillow.
And he forgot his alarm clock.

Months passed. February 2 came and a powerful, icy wind blew. Snow covered the ground. The lakes and ponds were frozen.

Groundhog did not appear from his den.
"Where is he?" asked Fox, shaking.
"I don't know," answered Raccoon, shivering.
"He's sleeping," said Otter, trembling.

Months passed. Winter did not go away.
Groundhog slept on and on.

"I can't fish," said Fox.
"I can't pick berries," said Raccoon.
"I can't dive," said Otter.

Finally Fox had an idea.
"Follow me," he said.

Fox, Raccoon, and Otter ran to Groundhog's den.
"Wake up!" they shouted. "Wake up!"

Groundhog came out of his den rubbing his eyes.
Suddenly the sun came out. The snow and ice melted.
It was spring.

"Is it time to fish and pick berries and dive?"
asked Groundhog.

"It certainly is!" shouted Fox and Raccoon and Otter.

And they all went fishing and berry picking and diving, with Groundhog leading the way.